Out of This World
World

Tales of Space

and

Gale Burnick

Watermill Press

Printed in the United States of America

Illustrations by Jim Odbert

ISBN 0-89375-790-X

CONTENTS

The Disappearing Planet

Day was ending on the moon. The sun dropped swiftly below the horizon. In its place, hundreds of stars came into view.

Steve Carey, an assistant scientist at Moon Base 5, sat down at the giant telescope with which he searched the sky each night. He began working the controls.

The telescope turned toward that area of space where Pluto gleamed. Earlier, Steve had spotted something there he had never seen before. Now, he leaned closer to the screen and stared. "There it is again," he said.

Steve picked up the phone. He listened for the click at the other end. Then he said, "Mark, come quickly. I want you to look at this right away!"

"In a moment," Mark replied. "I've got to punch these new figures into the computer."

"Hurry!" Steve shouted into the phone and hung up.

Within a few moments, Mark arrived. Steve was still staring into the

Steve had spotted something he had never seen before.

telescope. "What have you got this time, Steve?" Mark asked.

"It looks like a new planet!" Steve said. "But it appears and disappears. I've never seen anything like it."

Mark seemed interested. "Let me have a look. Hmmm . . . I see what you mean. Let's call Central Command. Perhaps they will check into it," he suggested.

"That's a good idea," Steve said. He stared at the strange, blinking light beyond the orbit of Pluto.

The next day, Central Command gave Steve and Mark orders to investigate. That night, a small rocket blasted off from Moon Base 5 and sped toward the disappearing planet. Mark and Steve were its only passengers.

The two scientists were heading for a

region of space never explored before. It was believed that nothing existed there. So, even at Central Command, the new planet remained a mystery.

"Can you get a fix on it, Mark?" Steve asked.

Mark was bent over the radar screen. He was trying to locate the exact position of the planet. "I don't know," he said. "One moment, it's there. And the next moment, it's gone. Wait. Yes, that's a flickering light. I've got it!"

Mark fed new figures into the ship's computer. The ship now held a steady course straight for the strange planet. "Landing will occur in twelve hours," Mark announced at last.

"You know, Steve," said Mark. "The way that light keeps blinking makes me wonder. Maybe it's a signal—a message of some sort."

Steve was silent for a moment. Then he said, "You could be right. Why don't we get the computer working on it? If it is a message, we really should decode it before we investigate."

Mark set to work. He remained hunched over the computer for hours. But the code was hard to break.

Meanwhile, their small spaceship sped past the planets of the solar system. Finally, distant Pluto spun away behind them.

"Make ready to land," Mark commanded. The ship fired its front rockets. Slowing down, it dropped toward the planet below.

"Are you sure we should go out there?" Steve asked. "We haven't decoded the message—if it's a message at all."

Their small spaceship sped past the planets
of the solar system.

"We'll find out what it is soon enough," Mark replied.

The two men put on their space suits. They checked their radios and oxygen. Then they left the ship.

Flat, barren land stretched all around them. No mountains, no deserts, no seas, no plants—nothing broke the planet's smooth surface.

Then it happened again. A brilliant white light flashed through the darkness. For a moment, the light was blinding. Then the blackness of space returned. But this time, the men had noticed something different.

"Did you see that?" Steve said suddenly. "The light came from *inside* the planet!"

"Whatever it is, it came from over there. Let's go!" Mark replied. They both began walking towards a spot in the distance.

Soon, they stood at the edge of what looked like a huge glass lake. Steve shouted into his radio. "You can see through the surface—right down into the planet itself!"

"I just don't believe this," Mark cried. "This isn't a planet at all. It's a space-ship! That's an atomic engine down there. The light is coming from the engine."

"A ship," Steve repeated. "But who is flying it?"

"I don't know," said Mark. "But the next blast is due any moment. Turn around, quickly. Hide your eyes!" The blazing light shot into space again.

This time, though, the entire ship shook. When darkness returned, both

"You can see through the surface—right down into the planet itself!"

Steve and Mark were rushing back to their tiny rocket.

The computer on board the rocket was flashing. Mark and Steve read the message that had just been decoded.

Ship breaking down.
We are in danger.
Help us.

Outside, cracks appeared in the giant ship's smooth, metal surface. "It'll blow any minute!" Mark warned. He pulled off his suit and jumped towards the control board. "We've got to take off, now, or we've had it!" he continued. He was still gasping from the run back to the ship.

Moments later, the rocket lifted off of the alien vessel and sped away.

"The next flash is due in five seconds," Steve said. He was sitting before the view screen. ". . . Three, two, one."

But his voice was drowned in the sudden explosion that ripped through space. Nothing was left of the giant ship—or of the smaller spaceship that had answered a call for help.

Small Planet

"We're going to crash!"

The spaceship was losing power rapidly. Dials were spinning madly as the ship fell. The pilot and copilot could do nothing.

"I think the planet is pulling us in,"

the pilot said. "Prepare to crash."

The ship skimmed over a forest, hitting the tops of the trees. Then it crashed deep in the woods. Both people inside were knocked out.

Frank, the ship's copilot, came to first.

"Are you O.K., Ann?" he asked the pilot. He shook her gently and she opened her eyes.

Ann looked around her. Most of the instruments inside the ship were broken. She wondered what the outside looked like.

"Well, I guess we'd better get out and check over the ship," she said. "We will have to find out just how bad the damage is."

"Do you think we'll need to wear the space suits?" Frank asked. The planet

The ship crashed deep in the woods.

outside looked a lot like Earth.

"I'll check," said Ann. She ran some tests on an air sample. "It's fine," she said at last.

They opened the hatch and went out. One look was all they needed. The front end of their ship was ruined.

"We won't be able to fix this with the tools we have," said Frank. "What do we do now?"

"We were sent to explore this world," Ann said to him. "Now, it seems as if we'll have a lot of time to do that. It could be weeks until anyone misses us — even longer until help arrives. So, we might as well see what grows here and check out any life forms."

"I'll check our supplies," Frank said.

Ann went back to the ship with him. It took an hour to clean up the cabin.

Then, they sat down to rest. Neither spoke.

Finally, Ann broke the silence. "It's not good. Most of our cartons of food were smashed. There's only enough left for two or three days."

"I think we should check the planet," said Frank. "Let's find out if there's anything out there we can eat."

Ann and Frank walked into the woods. Trees and bushes surrounded the ship. The trees were small. None were higher than ten or twelve feet. Here and there, they found some bushes with red berries on them.

Still, Ann looked worried. "None of these berries are bigger than a grape," she said. "Even if we can eat these berries, we're going to need a lot more. These aren't enough for one meal."

*Here and there, Ann and Frank found
some bushes with red berries on them.*

"Well, they're the only food we've found," said Frank. "Let's go back to the ship and test them. It looks as if it will be getting dark soon."

Heading back, Ann stopped several times. "I hear something," she whispered.

Frank shook his head. "I don't hear a thing," he said.

At the ship, Frank ran tests on the berries. "They're O.K. Shall we try them?"

"You go first," said Ann, smiling.

Frank ate one. Then he smiled, too. "They're good." Ann and Frank shared the berries they had picked.

The next morning, Ann said she had heard strange noises during the night. But Frank insisted he hadn't heard anything.

"Forget it," Ann said. "Let's get some

berries for breakfast, O.K.?"

They opened the hatch. There, next to the ship, were three big piles of berries.

"Where did these come from?" Frank looked surprised.

"I'll bet it was those noises I heard all night," Ann said. "There must be natives around. Maybe they're friendly, and the berries are a gift." Ann was excited.

"I don't know about taking gifts from strangers," said Frank. "If we've got friends, let's see them."

"Maybe they want to know if we're friendly," Ann said. "Come on, let's have breakfast. Maybe they'll come out while we're eating."

Ann and Frank started to eat the berries and waited for the strangers to appear. They didn't have to wait very long.

"I hear that noise again," Ann whispered.

"This time, I do, too," Frank whispered back.

Then, one of the bushes moved. Out came a small creature. It looked like a human, but it was only eight inches high. And it was carrying a red berry. Ann and Frank watched the creature as it walked toward them. It put the berry down in front of them.

"Thank you," Frank said, smiling. He slowly reached for the fruit and ate it. A lot of squeaky noises came from the bushes. Ann and Frank looked that way. There were twenty or more little people standing there. The one closest to Frank and Ann said something to the others. Then they all ran to Frank and Ann, squeaking wildly.

The creature looked like a human, but it was only eight inches high.

They danced and played around the humans. "I guess they *are* friendly," said Frank.

For the next several days, the little people brought food for Ann and Frank. They carried the fruit in their tiny hands, one piece at a time. It took them hours to bring one meal.

Sometimes, Ann and Frank helped the natives. Other times, they explored the forest. They often tried talking to the little people.

The morning of their seventh day on the planet, Frank called to Ann. He was standing near the ship's hatch. He was frowning.

"What's the matter?" said Ann.

"We'll never be able to go back," Frank said quietly.

"What do you mean?" Ann insisted.

"Look for yourself," he said, pointing to the hatch of their ship. "When we first landed here, I had to duck to get through the hatch. This morning, my head clears the top of the hatch by inches. It's the berries, Ann. We're shrinking!"

The Wind from the Sun

Earth was dying. For a long time, a hot wind from the sun had blown across the land. Now the wind began to blow stronger and hotter.

John and Tandy hid their eyes behind their hands as the sand blew around them. Few forms of life could survive in these terrible winds. Only the humans had kept on.

"How long do you think we have left, John?" Tandy asked her husband as they struggled along through the terrible wind.

"Perhaps four weeks . . . perhaps four days," John told his wife.

"Will it happen quickly?" she asked.

"That's how the scientists at the Center think it will happen," John replied.

The hot winds got stronger. A huge, blood-red sun rested atop a line of distant mountains. Night was coming on — the hot, hot night. As the sun set behind the mountains, huge flames rose into the air.

Years before, millions of people had

"How long do you think we have left, John?"
Tandy asked.

left Earth in huge spaceships. They had flown to other planets. But some had chosen to remain behind. They said they couldn't leave. Earth was their home. How many remained on the dying planet, no one knew.

At last, John and Tandy returned to their home. The few families that were left had built houses of steel to protect themselves from the harsh winds.

John, Tandy, and their son Brett began to prepare their dinner. Brett, now just fourteen, was a quiet boy. Because he had been brought up without many friends, he had quickly learned how to be alone.

Last year, Brett was allowed to take long walks through the night. Now this was impossible.

Brett knew everything was ending.

At night, he would dream of a great fire. When the dawn came, he knew his dream was coming true.

Now John, Tandy, and Brett sat around the table eating. With a soft chime, the vision-phone caught their attention.

"I'll get it," Brett said. He ran to the screen and turned it on. A young, laughing face came into view. It was his friend, Diane.

"Hi, Brett," Diane said, smiling. "Can you come over? Dad just came home with a bunch of old TV shows. He found them at the museum. It's the stuff kids used to watch."

Brett was pleased. Diane had been born on the same day as he had. They had been brought up like brother and sister. When he was with Diane, Brett felt like an adult. And he often thought, *Somehow I will protect her. When the day comes, I will protect her.*

Still watching her on the vision-phone, Brett called, "Mom, Dad, it's Diane. She wants me to come over. Her dad found some old TV shows. Can I watch them with her?"

Tandy came to the set and put her arm around Brett's shoulder. "Hello, Diane. I think we can manage it. The wind has died down a little."

"I'll get the car running," John called from the other room.

Outside, the night had grown black, and the hot wind was strong. The temperature remained at 115 degrees.

When John and Brett had left, Tandy walked into the bedroom to look at herself in the mirror. She was still young

*Tandy walked into the bedroom to look at
herself in the mirror.*

and strong and beautiful. She wanted to cry, but there were no tears.

Years before, when everyone was leaving, they had been asked to go. She remembered what she had told the officer that day.

"I can't go," she had told him. "How can I leave Earth? I can remember what winter was like. I remember snow. The mornings then were cold."

The officer said nothing and walked away.

From then on, the sun had grown hotter and redder. The ice caps began to melt. The seas rose. New York, Los Angeles, Miami, and San Francisco were now underwater.

Tandy heard the car approaching through the wild winds. When John walked in, he said quietly, "The sun . . .

it's just a matter of hours."

Brett and Diane were having a wonderful time. They watched all the old TV shows and laughed till tears ran down their cheeks.

It was not very often that they visited each other now. Diane's mother had even baked a chocolate cake for them with the last of her flour. When she came in, she laughed, too. Brett and Diane were sitting on the couch, holding hands and enjoying themselves completely.

That night, the hot wind blew stronger than it had ever blown before. Seas of burning sand rose into the air.

John opened his eyes. He reached over to touch the wall. But when he did, he pulled back quickly. The wall was hot enough to burn.

Brett and Diane were having a wonderful time.

John rose and looked out the window. The night sky was turning yellow. The sun had begun to explode. He turned to Tandy and kissed her lightly.

The great wind from the sun blew death across the land.

The Secrets of Venus

"Captain," I said, pointing at the view screen. "There it is!"

"Venus," the captain replied. "We've arrived at last."

Huge, round, and whitish-blue, Venus floated in space before us. It was winter on this side of Venus. Great sheets of ice drifted slowly over the planet.

"We'll circle the planet to find a good landing place. Stow all loose gear and keep a sharp eye on that view screen," the captain ordered. He began to prepare the rockets for firing.

For seven months, we had been speeding towards that bright and beautiful planet. "This will be the first time a human has ever set foot on Venus." I kept repeating this to myself while the excitement and joy I felt rose.

The captain turned to me. He smiled and said, "Make ready for firing."

We were coming in fast. Then, out of the corner of my eye, I spotted something on the approaching planet. "It looks...green," I said, "like a long, green snake. Captain, I think you

*Huge, round, and whitish-blue, Venus
floated in space before us.*

should take a look at this."

The captain stepped over to the view screen. He could see it, too. "That's strange," he said. "I was not warned about that."

I turned toward him and started to ask him what it meant. But he broke in and said, "There's no time now. We'll be landing in a few minutes. Strap yourself in and hold on."

We landed the spaceship successfully. After checking our controls, we put on our space suits and prepared to leave the ship.

"What's the temperature outside?" the captain asked.

I bent down to the computer to see the weather reading. "It says here it's a normal day — on Venus, that is. The temperature outside is 400 degrees. It's just hot enough to bake an apple pie," I replied.

"Save the jokes until later. We'll be safe enough in these protective suits. Let's go," he said. Then he pushed the outer door open.

An endless desert of iron dust stretched in front of us. Powerful winds blew the dust into fantastic shapes. And when the winds died, thin dust hung in the air, waiting to be whipped up again. High mountains rose up on the horizon.

"I've never seen anything like this," I said to the captain over the radio.

"Neither have I," he replied. We climbed down a ladder to the planet's surface.

The captain walked away from the ship. His shoes left deep prints in the dust that were quickly erased by the hot, rising winds.

"Come with me," the captain ordered. "We'll find out just what that green thing was."

A half-hour later, we arrived at the top of a small hill. And there it lay, the snakelike thing, circling the hill and stretching out for miles.

We approached it slowly. "It looks like a giant tree root," I said.

"You might be right," the captain replied as he bent to look at it more closely.

Tiny, stiff green leaves that looked like snake scales clung to the main root. "They're as shiny as mirrors," the captain observed.

"And as tough as metal," I responded. "You can't break them off."

Then, right next to the captain, a

There it lay, the snakelike thing, circling the hill and stretching out for miles.

long, green stem shot out from the main root. At its tip, a large, glasslike ball began to sprout. Thin green veins extended throughout the skin of the ball. The veins began to quiver. Inside the ball, something began to grow.

"Look...it's...it's got eyes!" I gasped, too frightened to move.

"You're right," the captain replied in a shaky voice. "And now it seems to be growing legs...and arms! It looks almost human."

The thing took on greater shape as it grew. After ten minutes, it stopped growing. The glass ball broke and the thing dropped to the ground. It was still attached to the giant root by the long, green stem.

The creature seemed to be a man. It lay in the iron dust, lifeless. Then, very slowly, its fingers began to move.

Bending closer, the captain said, "Look at this. The creature seems to be breathing."

I stepped closer. Just then, it raised itself up. I started back, surprised and frightened. "It's...it's you, Captain! It's got your face!" I shouted.

"Its eyes are opening. Let's get out of here!" the captain yelled back. But it was too late.

Already, the captain stood frozen where he was. The man-thing put its arms around his waist. The long, green stem wrapped several times around the captain's body. Slowly, it tightened around him. The captain moaned but did not move.

A few feet away, another green stem shot out from the main root. At its tip

*The man-thing put its arms around
the captain's waist.*

grew another glasslike ball. It, too, was covered with tiny green veins.

I wanted to turn and run, but I was paralyzed with fear. I watched with horror as the second man-thing began to form.

THE LAST MARTIAN

"We must hurry. In another hour, the last ship will leave Mars!"

"Dad," Paul replied, "I can't believe this is happening! Everyone is leaving. Can't the scientists be wrong?"

"Look, Paul, air from inside the dome

"In another hour, the last ship will leave Mars!"

is leaking out into space. In a few days, we won't be able to breathe. Please hurry with your packing."

"But I don't want to go. I just can't leave, Dad," Paul said, with a sad look in his eyes.

"But that's crazy," his father replied. "Look up through the dome. What do you see?"

Paul leaned back and gazed through the glass dome. "I see stars," he answered.

"Well, one of those stars—that one over there—is really a planet. It is called Earth. Do you see it?" his father asked, pointing up at it.

"Yes," said Paul.

"That's where we are going, to a new life on that rich, young planet."

As he continued to gaze at the planet,

Paul frowned. He turned to his father and said, "All right, you win." But an idea had taken hold of him. A decision had just been made.

Great crowds were waiting to board the last spaceship. It was easy for Paul to slip away and run towards the forest behind the city.

Paul's father got on the ship. He didn't realize that his son had gone. By the time he noticed, the ship would have taken off. It would be too late.

Paul reached the highest point in the forest. He watched from a hill as the last ship lifted into space with a great explosion. Below Paul, the city was silent. Above him, stars twinkled through the city's thinning air.

I couldn't leave. I just couldn't, Paul thought sadly. *Now I will be the last person to see my world.*

Paul felt tired from his quick climb. He sat down on the ground, buried his head in his hands, and began to shake with tears.

"Good-bye, Father," he whispered. Nothing answered him but the wind and a few night birds. Their cries flew over the tops of the trees and echoed in the city below.

As Paul listened to those birds, he dreamed of past times. His mother had been alive then. He recalled his third birthday party and the big cake his mother had made.

How pretty she was, he thought. Again, he heard only the wind and the birds. The city below him looked strange and lonely.

The night grew deep and cool as Paul

walked back to the city. *How odd it is,* he thought. *The street lamps are still on, but there is no one left to walk beneath them.* Paul shivered, but not from the cool wind. *I am the only one left.*

"I AM THE ONLY ONE LEFT!" he cried at the top of his lungs. His words bounced between the buildings and rolled back to him. They repeated themselves until they were lost in silence.

Paul's life changed completely over the next few days. When he felt hungry, he would just walk into any house. He would flick on a switch, and a warm meal would be served by the robot oven. He chose the biggest homes to sleep in. During the day, he would watch the image-reels. At night, he would walk around the empty city.

The animals and birds sensed that

"I AM THE ONLY ONE LEFT!"
Paul cried at the top of his lungs.

there were no Martians about. The wild creatures quickly returned to the empty city.

One day, Paul walked through the downtown area. There he saw a wild horse. The horse munched on the short, stiff blades of grass that had grown between the street stones. Paul also heard the barking of dogs that had formed into dangerous packs.

And all the time, the Martian air became thinner and thinner.

One morning, a strange thing happened. An electrical failure caused the city to lose power. The great buildings remained. But no lights, no image-reels, and no robot ovens worked. There was nothing left for Paul to do but go to the forest. The Martian people had first come from the forest, thousands of years before.

Paul took all the food he could carry. Then he began the climb. Soon he reached the heights from which he had seen the spaceship rise. He turned to gaze once more at the place of his birth.

I wonder how long the buildings will last, he thought.

That night, Paul found it difficult to breathe. He lay down beneath a tree and ate a little of his food. Gazing up, he found the planet his father had pointed out to him. It shivered in the thin air. As Paul looked at Earth, he thought of his father.

Maybe Dad is thinking of me now, he imagined.

Paul recalled the expression of love on his father's face whenever he had spoken to his son. It soothed Paul to

Maybe Dad is thinking of me now,
Paul imagined.

think about it, and made him feel a bit content.

Then, breathing with difficulty and feeling very tired from the day's climb, Paul fell into a peaceful sleep. The last air on Mars fled into space.

Gumdrop Planet

The mist cleared near the surface of the planet. The spaceship made a perfect landing.

"We're down," Captain James announced.

"That was easy," said Bob with a smile.

In a few moments, they were all at the portholes. Bob and the captain looked out of one. A scientist named Jim was at the other. They couldn't see much. The planet was dark and brown, and there was nothing in sight.

"When do we get out there, Captain?" asked Jim.

"Soon enough," the captain said. "Why don't you start checking the air samples? We'll check everything else. As soon as we're through, you and Bob can go out."

Jim went to his lab area and began working. Captain James checked the space suits, while Bob, the first mate, checked the hatch and air lock. Everything was in order.

Suddenly, the ship lurched. First it shifted one way, then the other. It sank several feet and then stopped.

"What was that?" asked Jim.

Bob ran to the controls. "The surface cracked," he observed. "The weight of the ship must have broken it. We're steady now, though."

"Good," said the captain. "Will we stay that way?"

"I don't know," Bob said. "Maybe we should go out there and check the surface ourselves."

"O.K.," said the captain. "You and Jim go—but just to check the ship. Exploration comes later."

Bob was still at the controls. He frowned as he monitored one of the dials. It was moving. "Captain," he said, "we're sinking. The dial says we're slowly sinking."

"Everyone at your posts!" the captain

The ship sank several feet and then stopped.

commanded. "We're getting out of here. Prepare for liftoff."

In moments, they were at the controls and ready for liftoff.

"Countdown," said the captain. "Five . . . four . . . three . . . two . . . one . . . liftoff."

Bob pressed the button. Nothing happened. The engines strained, but the ship was stuck.

"Cut power," the captain ordered. "Check our position, Bob."

"We're sinking, but more slowly now," Bob answered.

Jim went to a porthole. "It looks as if the surface has hardened near the ship," he said. "Maybe the engine heat did it. It looks hard as stone around the landing legs."

"What do we do?" Bob asked. "We

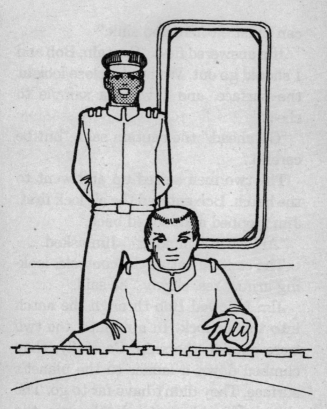

"Cut power," the captain ordered.

can't just sit here and sink."

Jim answered first. "Captain, Bob and I should go out. We need a close look at the surface, and I want a sample to check."

"Go ahead," the captain said, "but be careful."

The two men suited up and went to the hatch. Bob entered the air lock first. Jim stopped and looked back.

"Are we still sinking?" Jim asked.

The captain sat at the controls, looking grim. "Yes, slowly," he said.

Jim followed Bob through the hatch into the air lock. In a minute, the two were outside the ship. Carefully, they climbed down a ladder to the planet's surface. They didn't have far to go. The ship had sunk quite deeply into the ground.

Jim stayed near the landing legs. Their tops were all that could be seen of them. The bottoms had already sunk into the planet. Jim tried to collect a sample, but the surface was hard. He kept trying.

Bob was walking around the ship. "Maybe I can get a sample, Jim," he suggested. "The stuff looks softer farther away from the ship."

Before Jim could answer, Bob had walked away.

"Bob," called Jim, "I've got a piece. Come back." But he could already see the worried look on Bob's face.

"I can't," Bob answered. "I'm stuck— I'm sinking. This stuff seemed solid at first. Then it got sticky."

"I'll help you," Jim said.

"Don't come too close," said Bob.

"You'll get stuck, too."

Bob was sinking quickly, already up to his ankles in the muck. Jim glanced back at the ship. The hatch had been ten feet from the surface before. Now it was only three feet above it.

"Come back with the sample, Jim." It was the captain speaking on the space suit's radio. "Come back—it's our only hope."

"Go ahead, Jim," Bob said. "You have no way to reach me." Bob was sinking fast. He was covered past his knees. The ship kept sinking, too. Soon, the air lock would be blocked.

"Jim!" the captain yelled. "I have to close the hatch. Get in!"

Jim jumped into the hatch and closed it behind him. By the time Jim came through the air lock, Bob was stuck

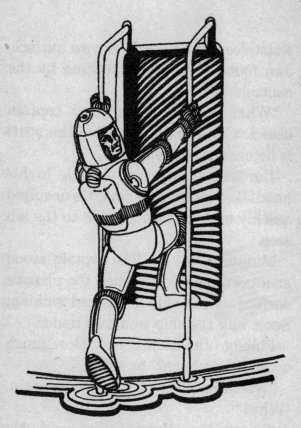

Jim jumped into the hatch.

waist-deep in the soft, brown surface. Jim found the captain waiting by the controls.

"What do you think?" the captain asked. "Can you find out what this stuff is before the ship sinks?"

Jim had the surface sample in his hand. "Let me try," he said. He unsuited quickly and took the sample to the lab area.

Minutes went by. The captain stood at a porthole. He watched the planet's surface as the ship continued sinking. Soon, half the ship would be under.

Finally, Jim looked up. "How much water do we have?" he asked.

"We have plenty," said the captain. "Why?"

"That's the answer," Jim said. He smiled at Captain James. "We can rescue

Bob. Open up the ports," he said. "Then start pouring the water out."

"What are you talking about?" The captain stared at Jim.

"The planet," said Jim. "I know what it's made of. Water will dissolve it. It's sugar, just sugar. This planet is a giant gumdrop!"

BETWEEN PLANETS

SOS...SOS...SOS. The spaceship's radio kept sending out the message for help. No one answered. The speaker was silent. The ship drifted through space. To save their last bit of air, the captain, his copilot, and the engineer slept.

The ship drifted through space.

Three weeks before, the spaceship's engine had failed. Since then, the engineer had worked to fix it. He could not.

The captain woke up first. From his cot, he stared through the window at the gleaming stars. *We are lost,* he thought. *We are lost and dying.*

The captain rose from his bed and walked to the control board. He flipped on a switch. *Maybe someone answered while we slept,* he thought. He rewound the tape and played it back. There was only silence.

The copilot woke next. "Captain," he asked, "has anyone responded?"

"No, no one," the captain replied, and he sat down heavily at a table.

The copilot rose to make something to eat. He returned to the table with coffee and sandwiches. But the captain refused to eat. Soon, the engineer joined them. He grabbed a cup of coffee and drank. His strength returned. He rose and walked toward the engine.

"It's no use," the copilot said softly. "If you couldn't fix it before, you won't now."

"I know," the engineer replied, "but I just can't sit around and wait."

"You're crazy!" the copilot suddenly shouted. "We're all going to die! It's no use. You're a lousy engineer. You failed!" He leaped after the engineer.

They fought in the hallway. The captain ran over and tried to separate them. But the two men were locked together.

Then, suddenly, the copilot stopped fighting. He began to cry. "It's all so useless," he said over and over through his tears. The captain led the copilot back to his cot.

The engineer, meanwhile, opened the door to the great, silent engine. Parts lay all over the floor. He had taken it apart and put it back together a dozen times. He knew it was useless. But he hated cowards. He wasn't going to give up just like that. He'd fight death to his last breath of air.

The captain felt the same way. For several hours, he had been checking the controls. The ship still had one more week of air. And a lot could happen in a week.

The captain turned to check on his copilot. He was sleeping quietly now. *Why us?* the captain thought as he returned to his cot.

Hours later, when the captain and engineer had both returned to sleep, the

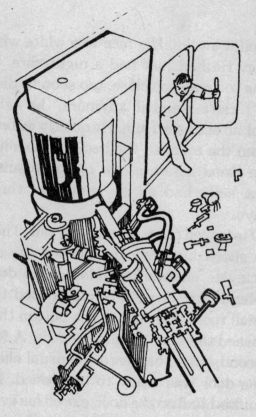

*The engineer opened the door to the
great, silent engine.*

copilot awoke. His face was white with fear. He had just had a nightmare. It was too real, too close, too soon to die.

"I can't stand it anymore," he said. But no one heard him. He quietly walked from the room to the back of the ship. He stood before a row of space suits. The suits had an air supply of three days.

He looked them over, one by one. Then he shook his head and opened the air lock. He entered and closed the door behind him. A rush of air flooded the small room. He pushed the button that opened the door to empty space. A few seconds later, he heard the usual click. The door was ready to be opened. He put his hand on the door, closed his eyes, and pushed.

A ringing bell woke the captain. He

knew what it meant. Someone had left the ship. The engineer was also rising. It must have been the copilot.

"That fool," the engineer muttered. "What if they find us after all? I hate cowards."

"Go back to the engine room," replied the captain. "See what you can do there." But both men knew it was useless.

Six days passed. Tomorrow they would have to put on space suits for air.

"Why doesn't someone answer our call?" the engineer wondered.

"I don't know," replied the captain. "But there must be other ships out there."

Suddenly, a burst of noise came from the speaker.

"That sounds as if it might be an engine," cried the engineer.

"Yes, but what kind of engine?" asked the captain. "I've never heard anything like that." The noise grew louder and louder. The ship began to shake.

"Look at that!" the captain whispered.

"I see it," replied the engineer. "I see it." A huge spaceship filled the entire window. It was brilliant, with streaks of lightning racing around it. It drew up beside their ship.

"Where did that come from?" asked the engineer.

"Your guess is as good as mine," replied the captain.

The bell in the air lock rang again. Someone was entering the ship. They heard a rush of air as the outer door opened and closed. Then the inner door opened and closed.

The captain and engineer looked at

Eight arms waved at them in greeting.

each other. The look of fear passed quickly across their faces.

An alien creature that looked like an octopus stood in the doorway. Eight arms waved at them in greeting. A strange voice rose from a small, black mouth in the center of the alien's head. "Do not be alarmed. We have come to help you. . . ."

Third Planet from the Sun

From fifty thousand miles up, the planet looked good. "It's almost as beautiful as Earth," I said, gazing through the telescope.

"Just about, Mike," replied Henry. He was my copilot and partner on this research mission. "The air is the same. There's water and animal life, too, according to these instruments. It's just the sort of place we're looking for."

"Do you think the United Nations would mind if we rested here a week?" I asked. I switched on the auto-pilot to take us down.

"They'd better not," replied Henry, as he stretched back in his chair. He closed his eyes and dozed off.

Our ship landed easily in a field of red grass. We were surrounded by a thick jungle of flowers that were as tall as trees.

"Come on, Henry," I said. "Let's see what we can find."

But when we opened the outer door and looked around, a strange sight greeted us.

The animals of the planet were coming toward the ship. "There's our greeting committee," joked Henry.

*We were surrounded by a thick
jungle of flowers.*

"It's odd, though, isn't it?" I replied, turning toward him. "They're not afraid of us. You would think they'd run off and hide."

"Look at them all. They keep coming!" cried Henry.

There were so many—monkeys with blue fur and red eyes, anteaters with long snouts that spoke to each other in flutelike voices, large birds with tiny wings, deer and more. At least, that's what they looked like.

"Mike, look at that one," Henry said suddenly.

I glanced to my left. A new beast appeared from the flower jungle. Since beginning this mission, I had seen some odd creatures. But this one took the grand prize.

It was about the size of a giraffe. It

moved on long, thin legs. And two tiny pointed heads were at the end of its long neck. As it approached, the other beasts moved out of its way. But not before they rubbed against it or touched its legs.

"They seem as if they're on friendly terms with each other," Henry said.

"No doubt," I replied, staring into the creature's four green eyes. It stopped a few feet from the ship. It was so tall that I could almost touch it.

Just then, Henry stretched out his hand. Carefully, he began to stroke its neck. Its eyes seemed to sparkle with pleasure. The other beasts became completely silent.

A half-hour later, the field was empty. The giraffe-creature had turned to walk back to the jungle. And the rest of the beasts had followed.

Henry and I had decided to stay around the ship. We wanted to see what the beasts would do next.

"It's too good to be true," I said. Henry and I were setting up the large transmitter that would send messages back to Earth.

"What do you mean?" he asked.

"Those beasts were just too friendly," I answered. "It makes me feel uneasy."

"Forget it," Henry replied as he worked out the exact position for the transmitter. "They are an odd bunch. Anyway, we'll only be here a week. Then we're off..."

That night, I tossed and turned. I had nightmares filled with the beasts we had seen when we landed. At last, I felt someone shaking me.

"Get up, get up, Mike," cried Henry. "Come with me!" Henry almost lifted me from the bed. He dragged me over to the door and opened it. "Look," he said, pointing. "It must have been the beasts."

There, just below the ship, the transmitter lay in pieces across a large area of the field.

"They must have pulled it apart, piece by piece," Henry continued.

"But that's impossible," I replied, growing more and more nervous. "We bolted it down tight."

"Bolted or not, there it is," replied Henry. "Come on," he continued. "We've got to put it back together again."

But the next morning, the same sight greeted us. The large transmitter had been taken apart and scattered. But this time, its most important piece

*The transmitter lay in pieces across
a large area of the field.*

seemed to be missing.

"It's no use," Henry said. "The crystal is lost."

"Or it was stolen," I added.

"Stolen? What do you mean?" Henry asked, looking over each piece and shaking his head in disbelief.

"The animals..." I began.

"The animals! You're crazy..." Henry replied.

"We'll stand watch tonight, and see what's going on," I suggested.

"That's a good idea," Henry agreed. "But we'd better be armed."

The night came on quickly. After the sun had set, hundreds of stars appeared in the night sky.

Several quiet hours passed before I looked over toward Henry. He was gone! I ran over to where he'd been hiding.

There was the chair, all right, and his rifle. But no Henry.

Just then, a strange thrashing sound came from the flower jungle, and I heard Henry scream. Then all was silent again.

From the jungle, I heard the sound of feet approaching. I picked up my rifle and ran back toward the ship.

Then I stopped. Before the outer door stood the giraffe-creature. Its four green eyes blazed with a strange light. I saw the light grow brighter and shoot out in a thin beam toward my hands. In an instant, the rifle began to grow hot. I dropped it and watched it vanish! Then the creature moved its heads toward the pile of parts that had been the transmitter. They grew red, then white, and vanished too.

*Before the outer door stood the
giraffe-creature.*

I looked around me. The animals approached in a circle that grew smaller and smaller. I began to run toward a gap in the circle when the giraffe turned its burning eyes upon me and I blacked out.

I awoke where I had fallen. Henry slept beside me unharmed. I tried to shake him awake, but it was no use. Then I looked up.

"What!" I gasped. "This is a cage. We're in a cage!" I rose and began pulling on the metal bars without result.

Off in the distance, the ship still stood, but a large streak of metal was burned out of its side. And all around us sat the many beasts of this strangest of worlds, gazing at me and speaking to themselves.

to hemorrhage during intercourse; from then on she feared sex. Your fear may have a very subtle form of expression. One man, in an attempt to master his fear of physical injury, used to pick up male prostitutes and pay them to beat him.

All these fears lead to false sexual goals: to be the expert "technician," having a one-sided relationship (everything for you or everything for your partner), having orgasm the exclusive goal of sex, keeping sex stereotyped because you're afraid to try new things. You completely forget the real goal of sex: sharing both body and feelings so that two individuals become a single unit.

A PROGRAM FOR SEXUAL FREEDOM

All your sexual difficulties may be due to fears. It is your fears that keep you from changing. You may (1) know just what these fears are; (2) incorrectly think you know what the fears are; (3) just know something is wrong but not recognize which (if any) fear underlies it.

As in any fear area, the first step in change is to identify the specific fear behavior involved. You do this first by taking stock and then by taking action.

Take Your Sexual History

The following quiz should help you to identify and gain perspective on your sexual fears. Write the answers (this will take time) in your Fear Control Training workbook.

SEXUAL HISTORY QUESTIONNAIRE

1. As a child, were you ever punished for sexual behaviors (such as playing with yourself)?
2. Have you had any traumatic sexual experience?

3. Did you feel guilty when you first started to masturbate?

4. What were your fantasies when you first started to masturbate?

5. Remember your first sex play experience.
   —How old were you?
   —What happened?
   —What did you enjoy most?
   —What made you feel anxious or frightened?

6. Remember your first intercourse experience.
   —How old were you?
   —What happened?
   —What did you enjoy most?
   —What made you anxious or frightened?

7. Remember a really good sexual experience.
   —When, where and with whom did it take place?
   —What was so good about it?
   —How did it come about?

8. Remember a really bad sexual experience.
   —When, where and with whom did it take place?
   —What was so bad?
   —How did it come about?

9. Have you ever had a series of bad sexual experiences? What happened? What brought them about?

10. Consider your current sex life. Rate each of the following areas from 0 (terrible) to 100 (perfect) as you feel about them.

     Fantasies _____
     Masturbation _____
     Anticipation _____
     Physical affection _____
     Sex play _____
     New or different ways of sex _____
     Intercourse _____
     After sex _____

11. In your current sex life, list the things:
    You would like to be able to do but cannot.
    Your mate would like you to do but you won't or can't.

You would like your mate to do but your mate won't or can't.

12. In your current sex life, show the areas of greater difficulty. Each of the following statements offers a choice.

The physical aspects or the emotional exchange.
What you do or what your mate does.
What you do or what you feel.
Whether you take initiative or your mate takes initiative.
What you expect from mate or what mate expects from you.
Not enough sex or too many sexual demands.

13. List the specific things you would like to do more or do differently.

14. List the specific things you would like your mate to do more or do differently.

15. What kind of things can your mate do to help you change?

16. What kind of things can you do to help your mate to change?

17. List the specific fears, worries or anxieties that may inhibit your sexual freedom. With each one show how and where it may work to inhibit you.

Your answers should begin to throw light on things you may do to gain more sexual freedom. You should also go back to Uptight Inventory—I in chapter 2 to see if any of the fears listed there apply to you. Again, remember that such tangential fears as the fear of darkness may sometimes be active in the sexual areas.

Identify Your Fears Through Action

Although questionnaires may be extremely useful, they also have limitations because you may not really know what frightens you. By taking direct and constructive sexual action, you may not only bring about sexual change but may also uncover previously unknown fears. Here are two action programs that may be used for both purposes.

EXPLORATORY EXERCISE I—
GET TO KNOW YOUR OWN BODY

Many people are strangers to their own bodies. They fear their bodies and the strange, new feelings contact may produce. By getting to know your own body, you may find fears you didn't know you had, may lessen those fears and find new areas for exciting stimulation.

For women: Get acquainted with your body. Many women never have. Look at yourself nude in the mirror. What do you like? What don't you like? Practice using your pelvis. When you just lie there, it's devastating to your partner. Alone, practice using your hips. Bump and grind just like a burlesque queen. Take a hand mirror and lie down on the bed and look at your genitals. Carefully examine the clitoris, labia, vaginal opening and perineum (the area between the vagina and the rectum). How does this make you feel? Good? Or guilty, ashamed, anxious?

For men: Become narcissistic. Look at your body in the mirror. Flex your muscles like Charles Atlas. See how you look. Pay attention to how you feel in your arms, pectoral and abdominal muscles, buttocks, legs. Stroke different parts of your body: the sides of your neck, insides of elbows, nipples, abdomen, sides, thighs. Note what you particularly enjoy. Imagine being stroked by a woman or being kissed on those parts by a woman. Stroke your anus, testicles, penis. See what particular parts provide pleasure. If anything makes you feel anxious, keep touching that part repeatedly until you feel more pleasure than anxiety.

CASE

Martin R. came in with the complaint that—although he had no sexual dysfunction—he never really enjoyed